The Littlest Engineer

by Jean Edwards

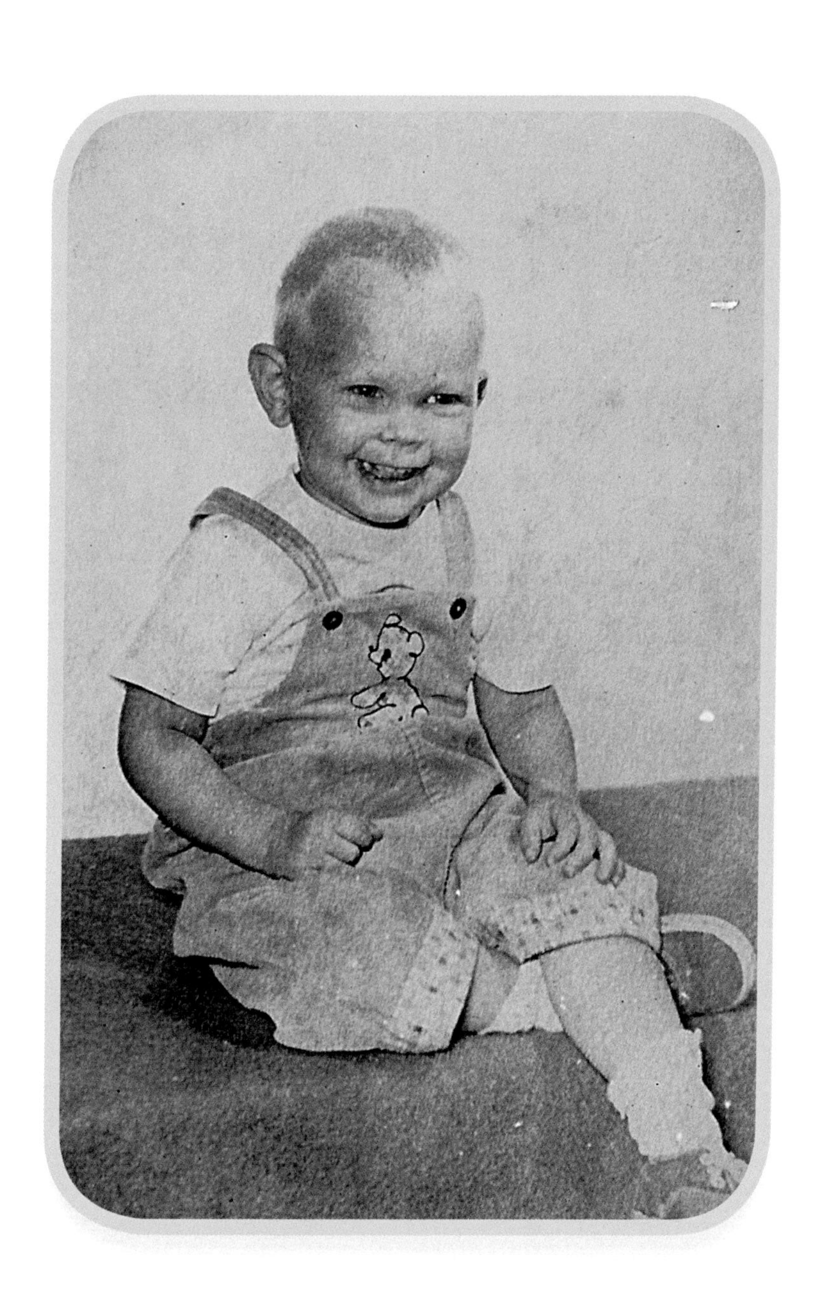

To order additional copies of this book, contact:
Xlibris
844-714-8691
www.Xlibris.com
Orders@Xlibris.com

ISBN: Softcover 979-8-3694-2964-8
Hardcover 979-8-3694-2966-2
EBook 979-8-3694-2965-5

Library of Congress Control Number: 2024919264

Print information available on the last page

Rev. date: 09/11/2024

Table of Contents

Larry's Poem

When my son was just a little boy
Every wheel he made a toy,
Every string became a cable,
Every book a drafting table.
Happy making woven webs,
Making space ships out of beds.
Every rock he called a treasure,
Watching him was such a pleasure,
Always filling childhood days,
Building paths to better ways,
Ever making something new,
Of every chore he had to do.
Making work into a game,
No two days would be the same.
Thinking back, I am amazed,
Recalling all his childhood ways.
Could I go back just one more time
And hold that little boy of mine,
And watch him play as he did then
Before he grew to be a man.

Jean Edwards (2013)

An Engineering Mind

The earliest clue to Larry's future became apparent when he was less than 2 years old. He enjoyed playing with pans and lids so he was allowed access to the drawer below the oven door of the electric stove.

Larry would choose from all the pans and lids and arrange them carefully on the kitchen floor; making circles, wheels, towers and blocks. No one knew what he was thinking, but it was obvious he was making machinery in his mind and displaying his vision on the floor with his pans and lids. It was the first sign of his future in engineering.

Tricycle

The Edwards' household was bustling with joy at Christmas. Under the tree was a shining red tricycle with silver chrome trim. Larry was too small (his parents thought) but Rose Anne was older. Little did they know that Larry had been born with an "engineering" mind.

After several efforts Rose Anne gave up on the tricycle and let it set. It was put out in the large storage room for later use.

One morning Larry was missing. His mother looked everywhere and finally heard a noise in the storage room where there was a large expanse of smooth flooring.

There was Larry, happily pedaling around on the tricycle.

Who would have believed a 2 ½ year-old could figure out the mechanism so quickly and happily, but Larry did!

Fishing

Larry loved fishing.

His first experience in fishing was while visiting his grandparents in North Carolina.

He was very proficient and always brought home lots of fish for his mom to fix for dinner.

The Clock

Larry wanted a clock of his own. Not an electric clock, not a grandfather clock and not a wristwatch. He wanted "one of those wind-up clocks" to put by his bed.

His father had seen a "Big Ben" wind up clock at a store, so when Larry's birthday was approaching he bought the clock. It had silver half bell ringers at the top that rang loudly when the set alarm went off.

Larry was delighted with his clock and took it to his bedroom. The next day his mother went into his room and there spread on his bed were screws, bolts, springs, cogs, wheels and various unrecognizable small clock parts, along with the metal housing.

Agast, his mother said, "Larry, what have you done to your clock?"

Larry replied, "It's all right, Mom. I can put it back together!" ..... And he did!!

Spanish Moss

Larry's father felt that children should learn to do chores at an early age to prepare them for the day they would enter the workforce when they were older.

The "chore" of picking up the trails of Spanish Moss that had fallen from the huge live oak that grew in the yard kept Larry busy. Under the fallen moss were loose rocks and twigs.

Larry had an idea! He would build a machine to drag the items to the back yard.

There was a sturdy cardboard box in the shed that he could use to make a trailer. Finding a length of rope he secured the rope to the box and then to his tricycle. He had learned to pedal his tricycle before he was three, and it had been his aid for many projects throughout his short life.

With the box for a trailer he picked up the stones his father had wanted placed in a pile near the trash cans across the yard. He accomplished all the tasks his father had asked of him, taking many trips in his "transporter".

Larry felt good about the job he had done and his father was pleased when he came home from work to a nicely cleaned yard.

The Pachyderm

The remnants of a pair of blue pajamas lay on a chair by the sewing machine. Larry's mother had used the material to make some much needed pot holders and all that was left was the neck band attached to a front strip that buttoned from the top down while it was part of the pajamas. Larry asked if he could have the strange article of cloth and it was given to him. His mother wondered what he was going to do with it, but she knew his active mind had a plan.

Larry took the strange remnant and disappeared into his room, later emerging with the neck band on his head and the front placket hanging down over his face.

"What are you doing?", his mother asked.

"I am an elephant," he said.

No more questions were asked. They went to the grocery store and someone questioned his appearance. "Shhhh…", Jean said. "Today he is an elephant." Larry was an elephant for a week.

A Pet Is A Pet (Grasshopper)

Larry wished he had a pet. Being a Navy family with eminent sudden transfers always looming over them, family pets had been out of the question, but Larry was determined. He didn't want a large pet like the mean dog next door that sometimes escaped from his yard and terrorized the neighborhood, but a small pet of his own.

Larry decided a large grasshopper would be a good choice, so he made a plan. Since they lived in coastal Georgia, large grasshoppers were not an unusual sight. Larry went into the house and found a cardboard box, just the right size to make a trap that would hold a large grasshopper, and he patiently waited by the large oak in the front yard for a visiting "hopper".

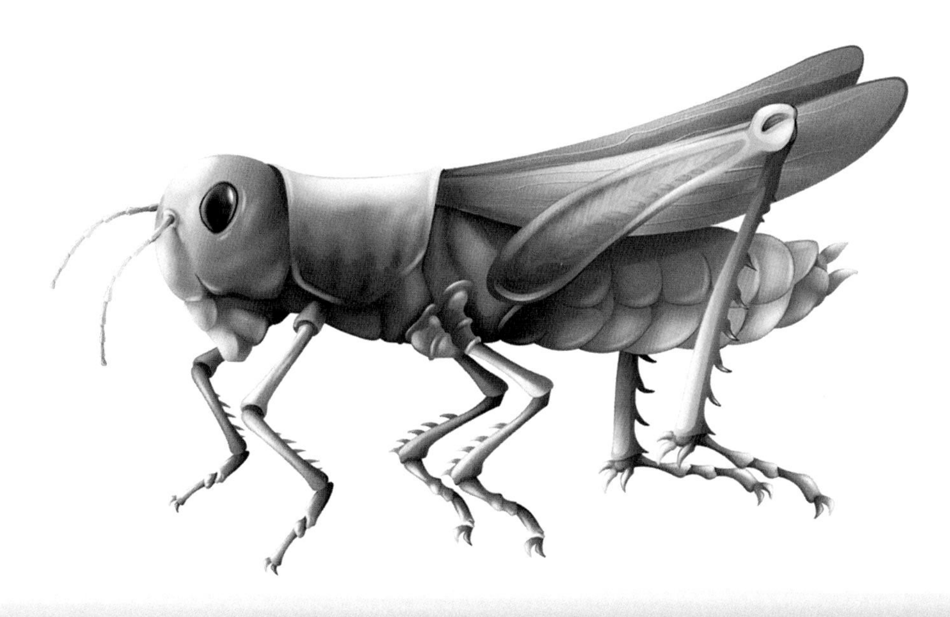

At last, a very large one hopped into the yard and "SLAM!", the box went down over him and he was trapped.

Larry found a length of twine he had saved from a package that had come in the mail. Very carefully, he made a small loop in one end of the twine, then slowly raised the up-turned box until he grasped the grasshopper by the leg, and gently holding the huge grasshopper he slipped the twine over the bug's leg and tied the leash on the captured grasshopper.

Aha! He had a pet on a leash! How proud Larry was leading his "pet" around the yard. The family was amazed at his ingenuity. He had learned to tie his own shoes at an early age, and now his knowledge had given him a pet. He kept his pet grasshopper for a week, and the whole family had enjoyed his visit. At that time Larry turned him loose.

Larry hoped his pet would always remember their time together and avoid being trapped in the future. He was glad he had turned his "pet" loose so he could return to his grasshopper friends.

Can a Conch Shell be a Pet?

Larry had not given up on having a pet of his very own. The family went to the beach on summer week-ends and the children loved playing in the water, digging in the sand and getting swimming lessons from their father.

Larry found a conch shell in the shallow fringe of sea water left by the surging of the tide. "What a neat shell to place on my dresser", Larry thought.

He watched it for a while and was about to pick it up when it moved. He waited to see if the incoming tide had caused the motion – it moved again.

Now he realized the conch was actually an animal carrying his house on his back.

Larry decided to take his great find home thinking, "I bet I am the only person anywhere that has a conch for a pet!"

Larry kept his "pet" for a week and it then disappeared. Larry decided it was a hardy and brave conch to walk all the way back to his ocean home.

The Porch Trap

Larry's mother often did sewing for people to supplement the family budget. One of her clients was a professor from a nearby marine research institute. One day he called and asked if she would make him a shirt from a piece of woolen fabric he had purchased. Jean agreed and he made an appointment to discuss the project.

The children had been cautioned to be polite and to entertain themselves while the professor was there.

A knock on the front door told them the professor had arrived and the children all settled down with their own projects.

Larry had never seen a man with black hair and a full beard before, and he decided that he needed to protect his family from the hairy giant. He carefully strung string back and forth in front of the door and attached the string to the pillars in front of the house. Larry announced, "I trapped him!!"

His mother took the amused professor to the back door and sent him to his car and on his way back to the marine institute.

Larry's mother asked Larry what he had created, and Larry said "I made a trap for the hairy monster so he couldn't escape!"

The "trap" was dismantled before Larry's father came home and the family had a conversation about harmless men with beards.

A Musician In Training

The Edwards family was a musical family with Dad playing every kind of stringed instrument imaginable and Mom singing in the church choir, and Larry was no exception to the musically inclined. At a young age Larry asked for a guitar for Christmas, and he received his wish!

Larry continued to play throughout high school and into his afterschool years.

High School Years

Larry could fix just about any mechanical device and when he repaired an old ham radio, the whole family enjoyed listening to the contacts he made.

Upon reaching high school he joined the gymnastics team and performed with great

athleticism in several events.

He was especially talented in floor exercise, and his precision was greatly admired.

When he had spare time he worked with his father repairing and rebuilding old bicycles to earn money for his college fund. He later advanced to repairing automobiles.

Larry ran long distance on the track team throughout his years in high school.

Singing solo in the school choir led to a leading roll in the musical "Flower Drum Song", where his rich tenor voice was well remembered.

Larry competed in gymnastics as a freshman in college where his precision of movement was once again acknowleged.

Larry excelled in a university drafting course which led him to an engineering job when he graduated. His precise drawings were marked with printing as impressive as his sports ability.

Larry's grandfather, Roger Fish, owned an antique Mercedes sports car. Larry's father purchased it from him for Larry's High School Graduation gift. Larry reconditioned the Mercedes from engine to exterior and to this day has kept the antique Mercedes in tip top show condition. He used his meticulous drafting ability to create the drawing of the beloved antique below.

Upon graduating from College with an engineering degree Larry entered the work force as an engineer.... of course.

He married a lovely lady named Mary, has 3 wonderful children, and now lives in West Virginia.

Printed in the United States
by Baker & Taylor Publisher Services